Heart of the Mavka
By
Allisha McAdoo
Jack Presby

About Kayla Wegner, the cover artist:

https://spookypeach.com/about1

About the Author: Allisha McAdoo
My other paperbacks are:

1. Dark Desires (a collaboration with Thomas J Kline)
2. Playthings with the devil (a short story collection)
3. Mr. Nice Guy (My first novel)
4. Your dirty secret (two of Mr. Rumple's stories.)
5. Night Terrors (A short story collaboration with J.M Swiger
6. Forever together (a vampire novel)
7. Yours for a price (Origin story of Mr. Rumple)
8. Twisted sideways (Asylum short story collection that ties all stories together)
9. T//Error404 (A revenge story)
10. Absurd witch (a comedy for teenagers under

the pen name Allysha   McAdoo)

11. Corpse Prison (a collection of stories that star Mr. Rumple)

12.No loose ends (The last story of Mr. Rumple)

13. Rumple Chronicles (The complete collection of Mr. Rumple stories)

14. Fatal Tales(a collaboration with Howard Carlyle)

15. Severed Dick Chili(a godless exclusive only story)

16. Absurd Witch 2(A sequel to Absurd witch under the pen name Allysha McAdoo)

17. Absurd 1 & 2 (A book with both stories of absurd witch under the pen name of Allysha McAdoo

18. I'm Cursed(an extreme horror story)

19. I know your secrets (An extreme horror short story collection)

20. Picture Perfect (A godless only exclusive)

21. Spiders, Toasters Rootbeer, and other prompts (My first ever prompt book)

22. Bibliophobia Fear of books (A godless only exclusive)

23. Book of fear (A godless only exclusive)

24. Naughty List (A godless only exclusive)

25. The wrong door (An extreme horror story)

26. Friends Forever (An extreme horror story)

27. Play Hearts (A godless exclusive story)

28. Luckier than you (An extreme horror anthology)

29. The pen (An extreme horror story)

30. Alura (A godless exclusive)

31. Beauty and Mr.Rumple (A sequel to Rumple Chronicles)

32. I eat people (An extreme short story collection)

Coming Soon

Mr. Yoinks (YA comedy with the pen name of Allysha McAdoo)

Heart of the Mavka (A collaboration with Jack Presby)

Mama and Mavka (A sequel collaboration with Jack Presby)

Verona (An extreme horror story)

My group

https://www.facebook.com/groups/1718802991696554/

My Facebook author page

https://www.facebook.com/allishamcadooauthor/

My amazon page (Where you can find my other ebooks on kindle and Goodreads)

https://www.amazon.com/s/ref=nb_sb_ss_i_4_6?url=search-alias%3Daps&field-keywords=allisha+mcadoo&sprefix=allish%2Caps%2C205&crid=1XQBXSJGNHP0

My author central page

amazon.com/author/allishamcadoo

My Godless.com page

https://godless.com/search?q=allisha+mcadoo

My Tiktok name is allishamcadoo

I started writing at a young age and have madly fallen in love with it ever since then. I have paperbacks available on Amazon and ebooks available on Godless, Pubshare, Nook, Kobo, Google Play, Apple Books, and Kindle. I have been published since 2017 and don't plan on slowing down anytime soon.

About the Author: Jack Presby
Already having written for the stage and screen, Jack's first published story was in the anthology Luckier Than You (an extreme horror anthology).

When not writing, Jack can be found on stage performing long-form improv with the Bright Invention ensemble www.brightinvention.org

You can follow Jack on all social platforms.

Facebook: www.Facebook.com/Jack.presby

Twitter: @jackpresby

Instagram: jackpresby

Book 1
The Heart of the Mavka
By
Allisha McAdoo
Jack Presby

Olena

My name is Olena, well it was at one time. Growing up, I had a strict Ukraine mother and an absent dad that was American. He was a businessman that sold guns to the militaries around the world. I had a twin brother by the name of Ivan who kept to himself for most of our childhood. He was quiet and loved to sit out enjoying watching the sky. My mother thought he was lazy and threatened to feed him to a Baba Yaga, a Ukraine witch that supposedly ate children. My mother, on the other hand, believed in all the Ukraine myths and legends. Every day she would find something to remind me of a legend. There were so many to remember, but she knew them all by heart. Every Sunday, she would try to trick me into going to church. "You must be blessed, you don't want to end up as a Mavka." She would say every Sunday. I rolled my eyes. "Mom relax, Mavkas were children who weren't blessed and died too young. I am almost 16 years old. Besides, I can't this Sunday. I am going on a date with Nikolai." I knew she hated Nikolai. I didn't really care. None of the legends she ever harped about were real. Nikolai and I were planning on running away after I turned 17 to go travel. We wanted to marry in a big cathedral on the France border. "Ay! No no no no! You need to get blessed. You'll end up as Mavka. He is no good for you! He is an Azhdaya!" I rolled my eyes again. "Mom, that legend is about a demonic dragon. Nikolai is not a dragon, and I'm not going." I packed up the backpack that I took everywhere and tossed my brother Ivan an apple. He looked at me with a strange look in his eyes and gave me a hug. He always went to church with my mom and did everything she ever asked. It was never good enough for her, she still turned her attention to me. "I'll be back by dinner time. I love you." I kissed my mother on the cheek and threw on my headphones. I could still hear her protesting loudly over my music. Looking back, maybe I should have paid better attention. But I am getting ahead of myself. My mother was so protective over me, I was pretty sure she prayed for my soul every night before bed. I wish I could get her into more modern times, but she was very set in her ways. She was always being on her best behavior even when no one was looking, so she couldn't turn into any sort of legend. My father never worried about anything. I couldn't understand why my mother fretted about every little thing.

I wish she would have given Ivan more attention.

To my mother, however, Ivan was invisible. I usually picked the long way to walk to Nikolai's house. I loved the forest and the lake that was supposed to be haunted by the children of the damned. Something about the lake drew me to it, and sometimes, I found myself sitting by it for hours. The bottom had a sort of red glow that almost felt like it hummed when you looked at it closely. I am sure that if my mother had known where I walked, she would have had a heart attack. I doubt the lake is haunted, though I think it was polluted. There were no swimming or fishing signs everywhere.

Today felt peaceful, and I kicked off my shoes before I realized what I was doing. I sat down in my favorite place, gazing deep into the water as my feet dangling into the water. I was used to the water burning my feet, but it was something I could never help.

Ivan

Ivan picked up a long branch he noticed on the side of the road. He loved his walk home from school because it took him past this little glen in the foothills of the Carpathian mountains. Ivan stopped and put his backpack down to better examine the branch. It was a nice branch. Perfect for a walking staff. Or, maybe if he stripped the bark, he could turn it into a longbow. Yes. That was it, a longbow. He could use it to fight the demon dragon Azhdaya. As Ivan removed some of the branch stubs and sucker growth from his treasure, a sudden movement in the trees caught his attention. Ivan held his breath as he focused on the grove from which he thought the movement had come. He's heard of brown bears coming close to the road, but he was more afraid to run into a Eurasian lynx or wildcat. Or a wolf. His Baba always told him tales from when she was a little girl and the perils of the woods. The hair on the back of Ivan's neck stood up. He sensed a presence behind him. He got a chill like a goose was walking over his grave. Ivan turned around and held the branch out in front of him like a lion tamer would hold a chair.

"Who's there," Ivan said and cleared his voice.

"Who's there," he said—louder this time.

He caught another movement. Something fur-covered. No, not fur. Hair. Black hair. It wasn't an animal. Ivan was sure of it. It moved on two legs.

"I see you there," Ivan said.

A face peeked out from behind a tree. A smiling face with the bluest eyes that Ivan has ever seen.

"Excuse me, young man. I did not mean to startle," the face said as it moved forward and out of the cover of the trees.

Ivan took this creature into his hands. He looked like a man, but Ivan didn't want to assume gender. They were teaching him all about that in social change class. Whatever they were, they were very hairy. Black hair covered every visible inch. The only other color visible was those blue eyes.

"I see you walk this path every day," the creature said, "I look out for you. I worry that they will take notice of you and."

"They who?" Ivan said, interrupting the creature.

"The Mavka. It is their feeding time. Spring always brings them into this glen looking for food."

"Mavka? You sound like my Baba," Ivan said.

"Oh, you do not believe in The Mavka?"

"Well," Ivan said, "they are Ukrainian legends, right? Like the Azhdaya?"

"I have seen many, many Mavka. I have helped many Mavka make their way to the other side. For you see, I am Chuhayster, hunter of Mavka."

Ivan shook his head to clear his mind. What was he hearing? Could all the old legends be true?

'Just please do me a favor," said the Chuhayster.

"What's that," said Ivan.

"Always carry a hairbrush whenever you travel near this glen."

"A hairbrush," said Ivan, questioning the Chuhayster.

"The Mavka will ask you to borrow one to comb their hair. Therefore, you must have one should you be asked."

The Chuhayster backed into the tree line and gave a little wave to Ivan before turning and vanishing into the trees.

Olena

The water felt pulsating under my feet, and the wind picked up just slightly enough to feel like it was humming against my skin. It felt like the lake, and the wind softly chanted my name. Even the stinging of my feet seemed to dull. The warmth of the lake and the wind seemed to put my body at ease. I felt like I was relaxing in a hot tub with no worries. My favorite band played inside my headphones as I drifted off to sleep. I should have pulled up my feet, but it was far too comfortable. I fell into a deep sleep, but it wasn't a restful sleep, no matter how comfortable I felt. I kept dreaming of chilling ice-blue eyes staring at me from the shadows that looked like hair. "I'll be coming for you, my Mavka." Sharp, pointed teeth smiled through the shadows like a Cheshire cat. "There is no escaping your fate." Those eyes seemed to tear through my soul. The presence inched closer to me, and I could see the tangles in the hair-like shadows. It inched closer to where I could smell its putrid breath on my face. The tangles were matted with what looked to be congealed blood. "Soon, Mavka. Soon." The presence smiled once more and then vanished as I jolted myself awake.

Screaming at the horrible dream, I accidentally ended up in the lake. Swirling pinkish-purple water danced over my head as I struggled to swim through the murky waters. The water felt like it was made from something like gel and cement. It smelled horrible, like dead animals. The water rushed into my mouth as I desperately tried not to scream. Every muscle in my body felt weakened and strained. After what seemed like an eternity, I was finally able to grasp the muddy log that I had been sitting on. My skin looked red and puffy. My lungs felt like they were on fire. I had lost my cell phone in the lake with my headphones. My feet were so swollen I couldn't fit them back into my shoes.

The wind that once felt so warming and inviting was now icy cold. It was too far to Nikolas's house, and I could not continue my regular walk. I turned back and went home. The twigs seemed to stick into my clothing and ripped my favorite shirt. I was too tired and sore to get too mad about it. I could feel my feet throbbing with a heartbeat, stabbing with each step I took. It was dark, and the wind blew through the trees with an eerie sound. Sucking in my breath, ignoring the pain, I began to run.

The whistling got louder and started hurting my ears as I ran as hard as possible. My breath kept catching in the back of my throat, and my side was beginning to hurt at the pace I was holding. By the time I got home, I was out of breath and sweating. I quietly opened the back door, knowing that everyone would be asleep. I quietly snuck into my room, hoping my heartbeat would not wake up everyone in the house.

My clothes were torn to shreds, and my body had erupted in blisters. I looked like I was cooked on the stovetop for too long. My feet especially, were as swollen as big as footballs. They looked worst than the rest of my body. No amount of makeup was going to be able to cover it all up. I snuck into the bathroom and began to take a hot shower. The soap and the hot water hitting my body made me want to scream. It was the fastest shower I had ever taken in my life. Each blister seemed to jiggle as it filled with jello. The pain was intense, and I had to stuff a washrag into my mouth to keep from waking up my mother.

I carefully dried off, making sure I didn't accidentally make any of the blisters rupture. I dressed in the silkiest pajamas and slowly crawled into bed. I felt hot, and shortly before dawn, I fell asleep. I woke up to my mother shrieking my name at the top of her lungs. "OLENA! What happened?" She was fussing about the condition of the blisters. She was wrapping me up with cold bandages smeared with Ukrainian medicine. It smelled a little like the American version of Vicks vapor rub. My entire body swelled even more while I was asleep. "I'm fine, mom. I accidentally fell into the lake by the construction site." The fear on her face told me that she wasn't listening to me. She lifted my foot which had the most burns on it. "Ay, you've been marked! A Mavka has marked you!" She was shrieking hysterically. I rolled my eyes. "Mom, for fucks sake, I fell into the polluted lake. There are no such things as Mavkas!" She was sobbing and praying while wrapping me up with the bandages.

I wished I had my music so I could drown out her sobs. They were heartbreaking. I didn't know why she got so worked up all the time over nothing.

Ivan had slipped into my room unnoticed to see what the commotion was. "What happened, Olena?" He whispered with his eyes wide. "I fell into the polluted lake outside the forest by the construction site. Mom thinks the Mavka now marks me." I said, rolling my eyes. Usually, Ivan would snicker and roll his eyes when my mother wasn't paying attention. This time, he looked like he had seen a ghost. His face was all pale, and I could see him visibly shaking. "I think you should come to church with us this Sunday." He whispered. My entire family was crazy. Usually, Ivan never said anything. To hear him suggesting church made my head hurt.

"I just want to rest," I said, closing my puffy eyes. Behind my right eyelid, I could feel a small blister forming. I could hear my mom still crying and carrying on. I just needed a good night's sleep. As I drifted to sleep, I muttered, "Love you both dearly. I am going to rest." I could hear Ivan whisper into my ear, "Stay away from the Chuyayster. He will hunt you." I drifted off to sleep, confused. I had never heard of the word Chuyayster. Why was he suddenly warning me of something? He never fed into anything my mother said. He just wanted her attention. As I slept, I could feel my skin tightening as the blisters grew. I could feel a blister pop on my back. The hot liquid was slowly oozing down my back, but I couldn't open my eyes.

Ivan

Ivan was daydreaming all through the liturgy. The priest's words were soothing and warming. Safe, yet, strong. There was a beauty to the Byzantine rite of St. Basil The Great. One that Ivan often enjoyed, but not today. All he could think about was Olena and those horrible blisters that covered her. He wondered if she would be able to walk on those huge feet. They were swollen and misshapen and full of puss. Ivan felt a nagging deep in his brain. There was a thought there that he just could not fully see. *What am I forgetting? Ivan thought.*

The priest's final blessing startled him into the here and now. The Liturgy ended. Go forth and do God's good work. As all Orthodox do, Ivan crossed himself from right to left and rose. The faithful started their slow shuffling towards the magnificent stained glass doors, and Ivan fell in step. He was still half dreamy as he looked around the naive. A figure in the corner of the transept caught his eye. The figure tugged at his brain, fighting the lost thought for attention. *So familiar, Ivan thought. I've seen that statue somewhere else.*

"Mama," said Ivan, "I'll meet you outside. There's a new statue I want to check out."

"I need to stop at the market, Vanni; just meet me there," Mama said as she continued towards the egress.

Ivan made his way through the cross-aisle towards the alcove at its end. He was sure he knew all the statues of saints here from Liturgy class. This looked different. *Out of place, Ivan thought.*

As Ivan got closer, there was a sudden blur of movement. People were jostled as they walked up the aisle, as if there was something moving them out of the way. Ivan turned and followed the same path. He was having a hard time getting through the parishioners and squeezed his way to the doors.

When Ivan finally exited the church, he thought he saw a movement to his left. He turned and caught a glimpse of a blur turning the corner. Ivan went to follow and was halted by his mother calling to him.

"Vanni, over here," she said.

Ivan stopped and turned toward where she was calling from. Ivan was torn between following the mysterious blur and obeying his mother. He hesitated, looked to his left and the corner of the church, and sighed deeply.

"Coming, mama," Ivan said.

Ivan was quiet on the walk home. He dutifully walked alongside his mother with the bag of groceries she had bought. He soon thought of the shadow in the alcove. Something about it was familiar. Then he remembered the Chuhayster. Did the goblin follow him into church?

They reached home and went inside. Ivan carried the bags into the kitchen and began to unpack them. As he was turning to put a can in the cabinet he thought he saw a blur of movement past his kitchen window. Ivan stopped and put the can down, then thought better of it. He hefted the can as he picked it back up. He could use it as a weapon if needed. Something was following him. He felt it in his bones.

Ivan walked and opened the back door, and looked. Their yard was separated from their neighbor's property by a six-foot-high redwood fence. This fence surrounded their house on three sides and extended to the pavement line. The back part of the yard was empty. Ivan stepped down from the kitchen into the backyard. He walked to his left and saw his cat on top of a trash can. He let out his breath. He didn't realize he was holding it. He looked down into his hand, noticed the can of tomatoes he was holding, and laughed. He turned to go back into the kitchen and came face to face with the goblin.

Olena

When I woke up, the room was dark and cool. I almost didn't want to move. Sighing loudly, I got up slowly. My skin was still a little bit red and puffy. The blisters had shrunk down but were still bothersome. I got dressed slowly in a pretty dress I was saving for a big dance. It was light and didn't aggravate the blisters. My mother was gone, probably at church. My father was on a business trip. I could hear my brother rummaging around in the kitchen. I thought I could hear him talking to someone but figured he was watching something on his phone. He rarely watched anything while my parents were around, but I knew he secretly enjoyed watching his shows.

I grabbed my backpack and snuck out the front door. I would go see Nikolai while everyone thought I was sleeping. I would sneak back in right before dinner. I took a shortcut to Nikolai's place. He was strumming a guitar in his room. He had that faraway, dreamy look in his eyes as his fingers strummed along. His fingers were long and played like they were filled with water. "Hi, honey," I said as I sat down on the bed beside him. "Holy Hell! What happened to your face?" Nikolai dropped his guitar on the floor as he took my face in his hands. "I fell into the lake I like to sit at. My face is a little red, is all. My feet got the worst of it." I slowly took off my sandal to show him. Right as I showed him, a blister popped all over his hand. Hot liquid splashed over his hand, and he jumped back away from me.

His eyes looked at me in disgust as he ran to the bathroom to wash off the blister liquid. I glanced at his mirror to see that my face had sunken into itself. I looked like I was a skeleton in the face. It was red and blotchy. My eye color seemed a little off as well. My jet-black hair looked stringy, like it was made from yarn. I waited on Nikolai's bed for what seemed like a while. Eventually, I slid my sandal back on, careful not to pop any more blisters. "Nikolai, where are you?" I asked, looking all through the house. Nikolai was no longer in the house.

I began to walk and once again found myself at

the lake. This time the lake looked beautiful and shimmering. Nikolai was standing there looking at the lake. "I am sorry, Olena." He whispered, not taking his eyes off the lake. "I can't be with a Mavka. I am going to get blessed by the church this Sunday." His words didn't make sense to me. "Oh no, don't tell me you believe in that crap too! I am NOT a Mavka!" I stomped over to Nikolai. My sandals were squishing loudly with each stomp I took. I stood in front of him so he couldn't see the water. "Don't say things like that, please," I whispered to him. I couldn't help tears falling down my face. The salt from my tears burned the red spots on my face.

"I'm sorry, Mavka, my love." Nikolai sobbed. He pushed me hard into the lake. I could see him running away. This time the water didn't burn me. The water felt amazing. I got to the surface and realized that all the blisters were gone. I looked really good; even my dress looked ethereal. I swam around for a few laps until my body felt amazing again. While I swam, I kept hearing Nikolai's words echo in my head repeatedly. The more I heard them, the more it pissed me off. I had given him my heart. In the end, he treated me like a piece of garbage.

I flipped on my back and floated along the lake as I watched the sunset. I was going to have to get revenge. There was no other thing I could think of to ease my broken heart. I wanted revenge. Nikolai was the only guy I loved more than anything else. More than music, more than my family, more than anything I could think of. I couldn't believe he fell for that Mavka crap too! It was one thing to hear it constantly from my mother. It was another thing to drive the only man I ever loved to church. The moon was now high in the sky, and I didn't really want to get out of the lake. It was so comfortable, and I wasn't cold. I knew that if I missed dinner, my mother would probably call an army to try to find me. I waited another ten minutes enjoying the water, then groaning loudly; I left the lake.

Even wet, my dress seemed to twirl around me as I walked like it was made from air. By the time I got home, I was famished. I could smell my mother's Solyanka, which is a sweet and sour soup. It usually had fish, mushrooms, pickled cucumbers, potatoes, and cabbage. It was one of my favorite things to eat growing up. My mother always put a special ingredient in it that put it over the top of any other soups I had ever tried. I never knew what the ingredient was, and never thought to ask. Knowing my luck, she probably made the entire batch in holy water. I sat down at the kitchen table and began to dig in. I didn't bother with the evening prayers. Usually, I would at least try to pretend to do them, but not tonight. I was too hungry. Water dripped from my dress, forming a puddle under my chair and feet. No one said a word to me as they watched me in disgust eating. "Something looks different about you." My mother muttered in between her lines of prayer. I could tell she felt uneasy in my presence. I served myself another bowl of Solyanka which was something I never did. Usually, one bowl was filling enough for me.

I didn't care that I ate my soup loudly like a pig. I didn't care that my family hadn't started to eat their food just stared at me in horror. I went back for thirds and fourths, clearing the entire pan. I burped loudly and giggled as I thought my mother would faint. My brother was acting strangely as well; he kept excusing himself to go to the kitchen. It sounded like he was talking to someone, and at one point, it sounded like he was throwing cans of food around the room.

"Thank you, mother, for the food; it was delicious," I said, finally feeling full. My mother usually made food that would last for a week, but I had eaten it all. I walked into the kitchen to find my brother standing on the counter tossing cans at a horrible goblin-like creature. "OH NO! IT'S THE MAVKA!!" It screamed. Ivan looked at me, and I looked at the goblin. "You are the second person today that has told me that! Now get out of this house before I get the holiest woman I know. My mother. Now get!" I was already getting a headache from the rage that was coursing through my body like an electric current.

Ivan stood there staring at me with his mouth wide open. The goblin turned and looked at Ivan. He muttered something under his breath, then took off running. "You could see him?" Ivan asked me wide-eyed. "No one else seemed to notice." I got a gallon of water out of the fridge. I gulped the entire thing down and then smiled at my brother. "Relax, bro; I won't tell mom. I wouldn't want her to drag us both to church." I tousled his hair and then went to go lie down. I wasn't tired, but I waited until the house went quiet, with everyone asleep. I slipped out and went back to the lake. I didn't bother to change out of my dress and dove right in. The water was beginning to feel like home to me. As I played in the water, I began to think of ways to make Nikolai pay.

I played in the water until the sun began to rise. I hated leaving the water but knew I had to return to the house. For once, my mother didn't say anything to me when I came into the house. She choked back a sob and continued to clean the house. That was strange. "Mom, I broke up with Nikolai," I said quietly. She didn't hug me or say anything. Tears were falling silently on her face. I tried to wipe the tears from her face, and she flinched. "Want me to help you with the housework?" I asked, grabbing a towel. She shook her head no and almost pushed me out of the way.

Everyone was acting weird. All I could think of was going back to the water. While no one was looking, I decided to return to the lake. I didn't care that I hadn't changed out of my dress in a few days now. I felt so pretty, and the water made me feel prettier. I could spend hours in the water plotting ways to hurt people who angered me in some way. Before I realized it, it had been weeks. I went home every night to eat all the food my mother prepared then I went back to the lake. I didn't bother to shower or change out of my dress. Eventually, Ivan asked me where I had spent all my time. "Come by the lake sometime; I'll show you," I said in a dreamy voice. "Nikolai called yesterday. He asked if you were doing any better." Ivan said, snapping me out of the daydream of the lake. "Ugh, don't tell Nikolai anything. He is a jerk, and I never want to see him again." I didn't add that I wanted to kill Nikolai. Ivan was saying something, but I tuned him out. I left the house while he was in midsentence. I couldn't stay away from the water. I had to go back in. The goblin was sitting on my favorite rock. I snuck up behind him and kicked him as hard as possible into the water. He was sputtering and yelling at me as he tried to paddle his fat arms. I couldn't stop giggling and dove into the water. "I told you to get," I said happily as I watched him struggle to get his chubby body onto a rock. He was panting and cursing at me. I tuned him out and began to daydream, holding Nikolai's head under these same waters. When I looked up, the goblin was gone.

Ivan

Ever since he chased the Chuhayster from his kitchen that night, Ivan has been noticing little changes to his body. Mostly his hair. He stood in the bathroom examining himself in the mirror and raised the scissors up to his eyebrows. They constantly needed trimming. He rubbed the stubble on his chin and neck. Ever since puberty, he was a once-a-week shaver at best. But since the encounter, he has been shaving twice a day. And it wasn't just facial hair. He had a full sprout of thick, dark curly hair growing from his chest. He stared at his reflection as he remembered the goblins parting words.

"You are now known as Lisovyi Cholovik. You are now the hunter."

Ivan finished dressing and went down to the kitchen for breakfast. His mother was at the stove frying potatoes in bacon fat. The aroma made him salivate. She turned to him and said, "Sit. I have your breakfast. Your sister was in and out again."

Ivan said nothing as he sat. His mother placed a plate of food in front of him and turned back to the stove in silence.

Ivan dug into his plate of potatoes and eggs. Silent, except for the sound of his fork hitting the plate. His mother was standing at the stove looking out into the backyard. She turned sharply to Ivan and spoke.

"Ivan. I am worrying about Olena. She only comes home to eat. I have no idea where she spends her time."

"She spends all day at the lake," said Ivan.

"Who can spend every waking moment at a lake? There is something else. You must tell me."

"Mama, please. You are worrying for nothing."

"A mother knows."

"I admit she is acting strange lately. It's because she broke up with Nikolai. But that's all. She goes to the lake to think."

Ivan felt bad lying to his mother. It was for her own good. Besides, he wasn't sure what was going on. How could he tell her about the goblin? About his warning? About him wanting to kill Olena?

The hike to the lake was pleasant. Ivan reached the shoreline and took off his backpack. He stretched his arms over his head and rolled his head around his neck. Facing the sun, he closed his eyes and let the warmth envelop him. A noise behind him snapped him out of it. He turned and saw nothing. Again he heard a sharp snap. Something stepped on a twig. He was sure of that. He wasn't alone here.

Ivan opened his backpack and took out his weapon. Felt its heft in his hand. The can of tomatoes had a dent from where it hit the goblin on its head. He put the can down at his feet and rummaged in the bag for the other cans. Soon he had a baker's dozen of cans at his side. With his back to the lake, he scanned the glen for any signs of movement. For any signs of the goblin.

Snap.

There. To the left, Ivan thought. Come on out into the open. You'll have to get past me to kill my sister.

Ivan stood there until dusk. And that's when things got really strange.

Olena

I noticed that my skin was starting to peel away after being in the water for so long. I saw Ivan in a distance going through his backpack and playing with some cans of food. I never understood why he didn't just pick up one of our father's many guns. He insisted he could take care of everything by throwing a can at something's head.

I heard the twigs snapping as someone was walking toward my brother. Ivan normally stuck to himself, and as far as I knew, he didn't have any friends. It had to be that stupid goblin. It was time for me to take care of it; cans of food would not do the trick. As I got out of the lake, I noticed that the skin on my hands had split in a few places. I would work on getting all that split skin off of my hands in a second. I snuck up to where Ivan was and saw his shoulders tense. The goblin jumped out, holding a fiery-looking javelin. He aimed it at me and was speaking in what sounded like gibberish. Ivan looked frozen, unsure of what to do. "Don't worry, Ivan; I got this. Go put the cans back in the pantry before mother sees them missing. Come back and meet me at the lake." The goblin tried to step in Ivan's way, but I grabbed him by his oversized ears. I didn't want Ivan to see what I would do with this goblin.

"I have to kill you! You are a Mavka!" He hissed at me. He was kicking at me and tried to bite me. He grabbed some of the split flesh off of my hand and ripped some of it off with one of his hands. I barely noticed the pain as blood dripped down my hand. A few of my blood droplets hit the goblin's hand, causing him to scream in agony. I rolled my eyes. "Seriously?" I was getting too hot and just wanted to go to the lake to relax. He was causing such a ruckus. I was so hot when I got back to the lake. I jumped in, taking the goblin in with me. The water didn't seem to affect the goblin's skin. I was hungry. I brought the goblin closer to me and bit down hard on his neck. Before I could blink an eye, I chewed through over half of his neck. My teeth seemed to shred through his spinal cord like it was made from butter. He went limp in my arms. I ate through his throat until his head plopped into my arms. His body slid down to the bottom of the lake.

I was going to let his head go to the bottom of the lake too, but I didn't want the myth that goblins could reattach themselves to come true. I ripped off his ears and threw them on the other side of the lake. His eyes I decided to eat. If he had no eyes, he wouldn't be able to find his body parts at all. They were sorta greasy and tasted like slimy marshmallows. I cupped my hand into the lake and took a small drink, which made the eyeballs taste much better. I started digging out pieces of his brain through his now empty eye sockets. The brains were actually green and looked like moss. I had to keep dipping my hands in the water to make the brain taste better. I ate the entire brain and then dropped the head to the bottom of the lake.

The water seemed filled with red glitter as the goblin slowly disappeared. It was getting dark; Ivan should be getting back soon. He must have stopped to look at the scenery. I was still hungry, but it was too soon for me to return home. It is always easier to come home when everyone else is asleep. The stars were shining beautifully when I noticed that Nikolai was standing by the bank of the lake. He looked horrified and disgusted. I didn't bother to say a word to him before pulling him into the lake. He was thrashing around, splashing water into my eyes. "I loved you dearly," I whispered to him as I began to stick my fingernails into his chest.

He was pleading with me, and I could see his skin bubbling from the water. I dug deeper until I felt the big squishy heart. Ripping it out was easy. It tasted sweet, almost like one of my favorite desserts. It was so delicious I kept eating him. I ate his eyes and brain along with the heart. Then I realized my grave mistake. It wasn't Nikolai that was standing by the lake bank; it was Ivan. I had killed my own brother. Screaming in rage I threw my brother's body out of the lake. I could see his spirit sit up in surprise looking at me.

There was no way I was going to ever return home

again. I couldn't stand to see the pain in my mother's eyes if she knew I killed, no ate Ivan. She would have the church kill me. How would I eat? After tasting goblin and human, I don't think I would enjoy actual food as much anymore. "What should I do Ivan? I didn't mean to kill you! I am so sorry." I whispered to his spirit. He looked at me then stood up. He straightened up and began walking towards the house. "Ivan, you can't go home. Mother will see you." I yelled at him. He stopped for a second and looked at me sadly. "I am so sorry. I'll find a way where you can go home, ok?" I pleaded with him. He didn't say anything but came closer to the lake bank and sat down.

"I will need help with a few things, I need a trap. Something to lure people to me. Evil people. If I consume more evil, I'll be able to help you out. Mother always said that those who devour the evil in the world are special. They can gain powers. I promise you, I will help you. Will you help me?" I asked swimming closer to him. He looked miserable and angry but nodded. He sighed heavily and looked at me. He said something but I couldn't hear him. I shook my head no and pointed to my ears.

He looked at me thoughtfully and then started to use sign language. Our mother didn't want dumb kids, so she taught us a few languages, including sign language. Ivan had suggested getting gold to lure in the greedy, singing to attract lust, planting fruit trees around the lake for the gluttony, hanging a political sign for wrath, mirrors for pride, something to make everyone envious, and a prize offered so no one would ever have to work again for the sloth. I signed thank you and that I thought it was a good idea. I told him to stay there and guard the lake while I went to get the things. Luckily for me, our father had most of those things in the garage. I hated being out of the water. It made me feel sticky and gross. I hurried down the path to the garage. I had to make several trips to bring back all seven things. Ivan pointed out where I should set up each item. My lake now looked as glamorous as I felt. I decorated myself with gold bracelets and rings. Surprisingly, none of them slipped off my hands. I wrapped a gold chain around my neck. I tore my beautiful gown to show off more skin. Then they began to dance slowly in the lake while singing. My mother had always said I had a great voice. Ivan looked at me unhappily.

I shook my head. This wasn't working. Usually, people don't go to this lake because it is polluted. "Can you bring me, Nikolai?" I signed to my brother. He floated around sadly and tried to leave the lake. He kept getting zapped by something unseen. I stood up in the lake and shrieked. My shriek seemed to ripple the entire lake and also brought out an evil-looking fairy. I grabbed her by her wings. "Let me guess? You are trying to keep my brother here, and you must kill me because I'm a Mavka now?" I sourly said. I was tired of everything trying to kill me. I stuck the entire fairy into my mouth and crunched down hard as I could. Her wings cut the inside of my mouth and tongue. Once I swallowed her, I felt more powerful than ever.

I stood up in the lake again and shouted," There will be no keeping my brother's soul captive or trying to kill me! I am quite hungry and will eat everything in my way!" My yell hurt my brother's ears because he clasped his hands over them. Several of the evil fairies came out of the shadows. They all were jumping on me and stabbing at me with their swords. Their swords left deep gashes in my arms. Angrily, I grabbed each one and stuck them into my mouth. A couple of them popped under my teeth like a grape. Smiling with blood dripping out of my mouth, I could see the invisible shield collapse. I signed to my brother to bring me Nikolai. He nodded, and I watched his spirit float towards Nikolai's house. I felt amazing even though the gashes made some of my skin slide off like my bones were made of snot. I started to sing and dance until a man stood by the lake. He was touching the gold coins I had scattered around the lake. "You like gold? Come here. I will give you all the gold on my body. It's worth more money than you make in a year." I sang out to the man. His eyes seemed to roll back towards his head as he stepped into the lake.

I could hear his skin sizzle as the water lapped up to his knees. With each step, I could see his pants shred off and his skin. By the time he reached me, the water was up to almost his chest. I ripped out his heart and ate it. It was not as sweet as my brother's had been. This one had tasted of pure evil and hatred, like burnt black licorice. I ate his eyes, enjoying the popping sound they made. The eyeball inside gushed with a liquid that tasted like sour fruit candy. I was so hungry that I managed to rip apart his skull with just my hands.

His brain was gray with bright red splotches all over it and had a rancid smell. His brain was diseased. Hesitantly I tried a piece of his brain. Spitting it out, I dropped it to the bottom of the lake. Usually, no one could see the bottom of the lake, but I could see every body part laying and decaying at the bottom. The sun was starting to go down. Ivan had been gone for a while. I wondered if he was going to return with Nikolai. But, I hoped he wouldn't bring my mother to me.

Ivan

It was dusk, and the woods grew cool. Not that it would have made a difference to Ivan. He cut through the trees like a wraith. He was enjoying this new freedom. It was as if he could move by just thinking. Still, he was troubled by the fact that he could see through his skin. It wasn't exactly clear but more of a milky murkiness. He held his hand to the light and watched the rising moon through his palm. The shifting muscles and veins made the moon look like a round, flat caterpillar as it rose in the night sky. He stood there like that for quite some time. Then, when Nicolai opened his front door, Ivan broke his trance.

"Ivan?" said Nicolai.

Ivan lowered his hand and looked at Nicolai. He tilted his head from one side to the other, as you would when observing something. He measured Nicolai up and down like he was seeing him for the first time.

"Ivan. What is it? What do you want? Is it Olena?" said Nicolai.

Ivan said nothing.

Nicolai took a few steps closer to Ivan. He looked different somehow. Paler. Sallow.

"Cut it out, Ivan. You're creeping me out."

Ivan said nothing.

"Did Olena send you? Does she want to see me?"

Nicolai walked closer to Ivan and got within ten feet when he suddenly stopped. It was twenty degrees cooler here. It was almost like Ivan was giving off a chill. Nicolai shook his head to clear his thoughts. This was weird. He started to speak and was suddenly unable to. It was like the air in his lungs froze. Breathing was getting difficult. Nicolai was beginning to get lightheaded due to a lack of oxygen. He felt woozy and nearly fell. Nicolai took a knee to try and catch his breath. His gasping grew faster as he tried to stand. It was like his whole body was being frozen. His movement grew more sluggish, and he thought he felt ice forming at the corners of his mouth where his spittle was landing.

Finally, he managed to look up one last time and saw Ivan move and glide his way over to Nicolai. Ivan put his hand on Nicolai's cheek and gave it a gentle pat. Nicolai passed out.

When he came, Nicolai was alone at the bank of the lake. He sat upright and ran his hands through his long black hair. *What happened, he thought. How did I get here? Ivan. Ivan drugged me and brought me here.* Nicolai looked around and saw no one. The only light was moonlight flickering off the lake. The trees all around him were encased in blackness. Nicolai went to rise and realized he couldn't. His legs were spread eagle and tied to stakes driven into the hard-packed dirt. Nicolai reached down to one of the stakes and pulled at it. He could feel it loosening. He continued to work on it and got it free. He then concentrated on the other peg. Using his freed leg as leverage, this peg came up easier. Now standing, Nicolai looked around and noticed Ivan standing on the water and not standing actually. Hovering.

Nicolai started to speak when the waters in front of him churned and bubbled as something rose from the depths straight at him.

Olena

I had been swimming at the bottom of the lake when I sensed Nikolai. My heart started to pound in my chest like it was made of rabbit blood. It always made my heart beat fast whenever I was around Nikolai. It was the reason I started to date him in the first place. There was something about him. I picked a piece of goblin bone out of my teeth. I swam to the surface just to see Nikolai standing before me. "You're here," I said, trying to get my heartbeat to slow down. It was beating way too fast, and I could hardly breathe. He looked like he wanted to say something, but I grabbed hold of him and pulled him close to me before he could. I missed him so much. I started to dance a little bit, forcing him to dance with me. I could feel his heartbeat through his thin t-shirt. I snacked my hand around his back and pulled him tighter to me.

I started to kiss him and could feel him trying to get away. I wrapped my arms around him tighter. "You shouldn't have pushed me in the lake, you know," I whispered to him. I could see himself getting lost in my eyes. I dug my nails deep into his back until I could touch his spine. Then I started to dig out little pieces of his bones from his spine. I would kiss him and then stick a piece of his spine in my mouth. The bone marrow was thick and delicious. Soon he became limp in my arms but was still alive. I had paralyzed him. Now he could no longer run from me.

Ivan was floating around trying out different things. I could feel the fear coming from Nikolai's eyes as I kissed him again. That was when I heard it—a twig snapping. Whirling around with Nikolai still in my arms, I came face to face with my mother. Her face was beet red with fury, and it looked like someone was squeezing her. "Olena! I warned you. Now, you have become the Mavka! You killed your brother too!" I had never seen my mother so angry before. She stomped her foot on the ground like a bull ready to charge. She was glaring at Nikolai and me with such hatred that I could feel the heat coming from her eyes. "Nikolai pushed me into the lake. I found my body down there." I said, making sure to keep my eyes level with my mother. I pointed to where I had found my body from the first time I had fallen completely in. "I told you! You should have listened to me! But, instead, you killed my boy because of your defiance!" She was getting herself worked up.

From out of the corner of my eye, I caught a dark cloud forming from behind her. "I can't let you live on this plane anymore. You have to be punished. Olena, you have to pay for your sins!" She shrieked at me, and the black cloud behind her grew. The cloud looked like it was her shadow but with a face in it. I turned back to Nikolai, who was trying to say something to my mother. I kissed him so hard that his lips split from the sheer force. I saw my mother step back into the cloud as I kissed him. "I will stop you, Olena! You can not remain here anymore." The cloud and my mother formed back into my mother. Her once gray eyes were now a dark red color. She no longer looked aged with wrinkles. Whatever she had done, she had made herself powerful.

I watched my mother stomp away. Still holding Nikolai and dragging him on the ground behind me, I followed my mother into the shed by the house. She left the shed door open as she pulled the sledgehammer from the wall. The wall swung back, revealing a small room behind the tools rack. The room was lit with candles in all shapes and colors. Stepping forward, I felt a zap of electricity coming from that room. My mother stood there smiling at me. "You can't come in here, Olena. Mark my words. I will be back for you." She lit a candle that was in the shape of a ballerina.

Suddenly, I felt like the air had been knocked out of me. She closed the door firmly behind her. I could hear a heavy lock click into place. I barely had enough strength to drag Nikolai back to the lake with me. If it was a war she wanted, it was a war she would get. I thought to myself. I looked around to see Ivan was no longer by the water. I grabbed a branch and whittled it to a point with my teeth. My teeth were chipped and bleeding, making it look like I was wearing lipstick. I jammed the stick into the middle of the lake and shoved Nikolai on it so he couldn't move. "You aren't allowed to die until I am finished with you," I whispered as he sobbed. The branch was sticking up from his stomach a little bit.

I kissed him again and saw that the water would keep him alive. The water lapped over his body like a seductive lover. The water made his skin-pop and sizzle like hot bacon in a pan but also made his skin have a strange glow to it. I began to dance and sing, this time making sure my voice carried to the villages below the slope where the lake was. If my mother wanted to take me to hell, I would have to eat a lot of people and magical creatures. I had no idea how strong my mother had gotten over the years and didn't like the fact I had been tossed off my guard.

She had called me defiant and was angrier because Ivan had been killed. She didn't care about the fact that Nikolai had killed me. There was no way I would let her stand in my way.

"Olena, please just kill me," Nikolai whispered. Angrily, I whirled around until I was face to face with him. "You killed me. Now you have to stay by my side for all eternity. So if I get dragged to hell, do you. This is because of you." Nikolai started to protest again, but this time I kissed him. I snaked my tongue into his mouth. I could taste his morning coffee from the day before he came to the lake. I bit his tongue until it squished loudly in my mouth. Then, with more force, I ripped it out of his head and ate it. "You can't whine or beg for your life," I said sweetly as I looked at him deeply. He was sobbing like a little child. Tears were mixing with blood as they dripped down his cheeks. Snot was sliding out of his nose and down to his chin.

I once more began to sing and dance—time to get ready for the next step of my continued existence.

To Be Continued……..
Book 2 Mama and Mavka are in the works; stay tuned.

Book 2
Mama and Mavka
By
Allisha McAdoo
Jack Presby
Copyright © Allisha McAdoo Jack Presby 2022

First Printing, Cover work done by Kayla Wegner 2022

About Kayla Wegner, the cover artist: https://spookypeach.com/about1

About the Author: Allisha McAdoo
My other paperbacks are:
1. Dark Desires (a collaboration with Thomas J Kline)
2. Playthings with the devil (a short story collection)
3. Mr. Nice Guy (My first novel)
4. Your dirty secret (two of Mr. Rumple's stories.)
5. Night Terrors (A short story collaboration with J.M Swiger
6. Forever together (a vampire novel)
7. Yours for a price (Origin story of Mr. Rumple)
8. Twisted sideways (Asylum short story collection that ties all stories together)
9. T//Error404 (A revenge story)

10. Absurd witch (a comedy for teenagers under the pen name Allysha   McAdoo)

11. Corpse Prison (a collection of stories that star Mr. Rumple)

12.No loose ends (The last story of Mr. Rumple)

13. Rumple Chronicles (The complete collection of Mr. Rumple stories)

14. Fatal Tales(a collaboration with Howard Carlyle)

15. Severed Dick Chili(a godless exclusive only story)

16. Absurd Witch 2(A sequel to Absurd witch under the pen name Allysha McAdoo)

17. Absurd 1 & 2 (A book with both stories of absurd witch under the pen name of Allysha McAdoo

18. I'm Cursed(an extreme horror story)

19. I know your secrets (An extreme horror short story collection)

20. Picture Perfect (A godless only exclusive)

21. Spiders, Toasters Rootbeer, and other prompts (My first ever prompt book)

22. Bibliophobia Fear of books (A godless only exclusive)

23. Book of fear (A godless only exclusive)

24. Naughty List (A godless only exclusive)

25. The wrong door (An extreme horror story)

26. Friends Forever (An extreme horror story)

27. Play Hearts (A godless exclusive story)

28. Luckier than you (An extreme horror anthology)

29. The pen (An extreme horror story)

30. Alura (A godless exclusive)

31. Beauty and Mr.Rumple (A sequel to Rumple Chronicles)

32. I eat people (An extreme short story collection)

33. Cryptid Carnage (An anthology with my story Wendigo)

34. Heart of the Mavka (A collaboration with Jack Presby)

35. Painted smiles (An extreme horror story)

36. Revenge (A collection of revenge stories)

37. Twisted Images (A collaboration with Jack Presby)

38. Pillow Talk (A godless exclusive)

39. Twisted Images (A pubshare exclusive collaboration with Jack Presby)

40. Mama and Mavka (A sequel collaboration with Jack Presby)

41. Mavka Collection (Both stories in one book, collaboration with Jack Presby)

My group
https://www.facebook.com/
groups/1718802991696554/
My Facebook author page
https://www.facebook.com/allishamcadooauthor/
My amazon page (Where you can find my other ebooks on kindle and Goodreads)
https://www.amazon.com/s/ref=nb_sb_ss_i_4_6?
url=search-alias%3Daps&field-keywords=allisha
+mcadoo&sprefix=allish%2Caps
%2C205&crid=1XQBXSJGNHP0
My author central page
amazon.com/author/allishamcadoo
My Godless.com page
https://godless.com/search?q=allisha+mcadoo

My Tiktok name is allishamcadoo

I started writing at a young age and have madly fallen in love with it ever since then. I have paperbacks available on Amazon and ebooks available on Godless, Pubshare, Nook, Kobo, Google Play, Apple Books, and Kindle. I have been published since 2017 and don't plan on slowing down anytime soon.

About the Author Jack Presby:
About the Author : Jack Presby

Already having written for the stage and screen, Jack's first published story was in the anthology Luckier Than You (an extreme horror anthology).

When not writing, Jack can be found on stage performing long-form improv with the Bright Invention ensemble www.brightinvention.org

You can follow Jack on all social platforms.

Facebook: www.Facebook.com/Jack.presby

Twitter: @jackpresby

Instagram: jackpresby

Mama / Alona

My name is Alona. I am the mother of Olena and Ivan, my two angels from the heavens above. Ivan was a good boy, but to be honest. I overlooked him most of the time. Not that I did it on purpose, but my daughter Olena was stubborn and rebellious. When she was a little girl, I knew right down to my bones that she would be the one I would need the most divine help.

Olena was a difficult child, always rebutting the rules. Every Sunday, I would take her to Sunday school. Every Sunday, she found some way or another to get herself out of the class. I knew I had to find some greater power to help me. I knew by the time she turned six years old. Her destiny was a fate worse than death. I did everything in my power to keep that from happening. Ultimately, she turns into a Mavka, kills her brother, and holds a soul in limbo. Poor Nikolai, I never liked him, but he doesn't deserve what she is doing.

I belonged to a secret organization that didn't just rely on the divine power to help. When Olena was ten years old, she broke the preacher's daughter's arm. She bent it into several angles enough to break it six times. She smiled sweetly as the preacher's daughter's blood dripped from her chin. When I asked her why she did what she did, she shrugged. "I just got tired of her voice droning on." She giggled. I was approached in the hospital as the doctor set the girl's arm. "Hello, Alona. I think you will need this more than anyone else in the congregation. My name is Nairobi. We are part of an organization that will help you with your daughter. She is not destined for something great. You must know that." She smiled sweetly and handed me a business card. Just like that, I was hooked.

Every day right before school would end, we would have meetings. Some of the men turned my shed into a war preparedness room. I was given plenty of instructions on what to do when the time came. I had prayed every night to help keep my precious Olena from turning into something worse. But unfortunately, my prayers fell on deaf ears. As Nairobi once said, God would sit this fight out. I saw with my own eyes what Olena had become. I sealed myself into the chamber, watching her cold, dead eyes gaze at me in defiance. Even dead, her defiance was a fire that would be hard to put out.

I waited until all the candles blew out by themselves, plunging me into complete darkness. The darkness felt so cold that even my bones were starting to ache. A part of me wished I was younger for the task I would have to do. This world was messed up as it is; it didn't need a Mavka as well. I knew in my heart that Olena wouldn't just stick to men; no one would be safe from her. People were naturally drawn to sins, desires, and chaos. They were easy targets.

I stifled a sob that was threatening to come out. There wasn't time to sob or to feel badly about my mission. I didn't need the light to exit the chambers; I had walked its hallways so many times over the years I knew it all by heart. I opened the door to see Olena had left to go back to the lake. A blood trail and matted leaves were what she left behind. I needed to get my husband, Bosko; he would have to bring me a few ingredients from his workplace. His work had started to experiment with different biological warfare in secret. I only knew of it, thanks to Nairobi.

I walked into the house quietly. My head was spinning, and I felt weak in my knees. I got a glass of water from the tap water once it turned clear. The old pipes in the house made the water the color of rust for a few seconds before good water would come. I took a deep breath and stepped into Ivan's room. I was going to miss him, and I regretted not spending much time with him. "In our next life, Ivan, I promise to be a better mother to you," I whispered to the empty room. Tears quietly slid down my cheeks as I packed up all of Ivan's things. I put it all into the attic with a note that read that Olena had turned into a Mavka and killed him.

Next, I moved to Olena's room. Sighing heavily, the tears stopped. Her room was such a mess. My anger grew. I didn't bother to save almost anything of her things. I saved a few pictures and a few pieces of jewelry she always wore until the day she came home with blisters. I kept her hairbrush with the hairs still intact in the bristles. Everything else, I bagged into heavy-duty trash bags. It took a couple of hours, and my back was killing me from all the hard work. I was not in the best shape; after all, I was in my 50s. With both rooms cleaned out completely, I locked both doors with a heavy-duty padlock. "Neither of you is welcome to come home now," I whispered at the thick locks in my hands. With shaking hands, I threw the keys away.

I carefully packed the things in Olena's room into a purple silk bag. Those would be the things I would need to help drag her to Hell. I waited until Bosko came home from work. "You need to sit down," I said to him. I had rehearsed what I was going to say to him over and over again.

"There's no need Alona. I think after 20 years of marriage, it's time I came clean. I've been sleeping with my secretary, Dolores, for about ten years now.

I am not in my position in the company; in fact, I was made CEO. I didn't bother to tell you because of the extra money I made I gave to Dolores. She is moving back to the states. My company and I are going with her. I don't care about the kids; they are old enough to make their own choices. I'm not sorry for what I've done. I'm just sorry it took so long to come clean. Your constant ramblings about myths and legends drove me crazy. Dolores was there with open arms. I worked later and later into the evenings just so that way I wouldn't have to interact with you much. I already packed my things earlier today and had them shipped to the states. I leave in twenty minutes. I won't give you a divorce as far as anyone knows; you will be dead." Bosko said in a cruel tone of voice.

He lit a match and threw it onto the old frayed rug that ran almost around the entire house. "Goodbye, Alona." He said simply as he tossed a bottle of booze at my feet. The fire ignited the broken bottle as quickly as a child lapping up ice cream melting. Fire licked at my legs like an angry lover. Tears had been falling down my cheeks so quickly that they left a sticky trail down to my chin. Bosko slammed the front door as more things went up in flame. I could hear the deadbolt click into place.

For a second, I couldn't decide whether or not to go after him and kill him or to go after Olena. The flames were up to my knees now, and I could hear my skin sizzling under the extreme heat. I looked around the house, trying to memorize all the memories as I began to get up from the chair. I ran to the kitchen and yanked off my dress. I soaked it with water and then put it back on me. Then I took off running. I grabbed the purple silk bag and then tried to make my way to the attic. I needed a couple of pictures of Ivan if I was going to help him after Olena was in Hell.

I didn't make it up to the attic before it collapsed. Chunks of broken, burnt wood started to rain down all around me. Everything that used to be in the attic was falling down in a burnt mess like a child throwing a tantrum. The air filled with dark black smoke, and it was getting harder to breathe. I tried to get out the front door, but the fire had melted the lock. Looking around, I couldn't find anything but a can of food that wasn't on fire. I took the can of tomatoes and chucked it out the window. The sound of glass shattering as the fire exploded made my ears ring.

Somehow, I managed to climb out the window I had broken. I cut my leg up pretty well and could feel it stinging through the flames that were still on my body. I dropped to the ground and began to roll around in the grass. The grass was dry because we hadn't had rain in so long, and the fire spread. Desperate, I took off running until I was at Bosko's koi pond. Without thinking about it, I jumped into the water. The heat from my body alone killed any fish that came into contact with me. Bosko had loved those koi fish more than he ever loved me; it was only payback I killed some of them. I crawled out of the water with my body still smoking. I brought the silk, purple bag back into the war chamber. I called Nairobi and left a message on her machine about what happened. I lay down on the nice cool concrete and closed my eyes.

Ivan

Ivan became self-aware for the second time shortly after midnight on October 30th of that year. It was like a light switch was turned on in his head. A quick flick, and, voila, here he was.

Ivan was gliding through the woods, leaving a trail of frost on everything he passed. The larch he passed through was flash-frozen in the middle of its trunk. Late blooming flowers became suspended in time, never fully opened, and had their nectar suckled, and thus died unfulfilled. Much like Ivan. He stood in a small clearing staring at the hunter's moon, basking in its glow. He could see the blood coursing in his veins through his transparent skin. He could see the full moon's tidal effect on it. How the blood enjoyed the pull of gravity. His shredded clothing had nearly all fallen off, and he could easily see his organs through his skin. He watched in fascination his heart as it pumped and pushed and pulsated. The rhythm was soothing and almost musical. His trance was broken by a branch snapping to his left. In his peripheral, he noticed a huge dark shape. He turned to face the intrusion but saw nothing. Nothing human.

A cloud was staring at him. A huge dark cloud. Ivan could sense the cloud was trying to probe his mind. He blocked the probe and sent one of his own back. The cloud seemed to wince if a cloud could wince, and Ivan walked close to it.

The cloud doubled in size at Ivan's approach as if to loom over him. Ivan walked close enough to reach into it, raised his hand, and stopped.

"It's not too late for you," said the cloud in a thunderous voice.

Ivan said nothing.

"Your mama has sent me to guide you and protect you."

Ivan said nothing.

"For you are elemental now," the cloud said, "your immortal soul is in jeopardy unless your mama can kill the Mavka."

Ivan turned his face up at the cloud and noticed the small face looking down at him. So benevolent. So cherub-like.

"Protect me from what exactly," said Ivan.

"Other elementals. You are in transition. There is no set element for you yet. Fire is the worst one. Fire has no good side. The other elements, well, they have good and bad sides. Why even us Coriolis can be bad?

"Coriolis," Ivan asked.

"We are the wind," said the cloud.

"Why should I care," said Ivan.

"The others will try to exploit your new

powers. They will promise you your soul. Well, they can't. See, elementals, although long-lasting, have no soul. They forfeit the right to a soul in return for longevity. So as a result, some elementals are in constant battle with humans because they are jealous of them being immortal."

"What would they want with me? I'm neither earth, water nor fire. And I'm certainly not wind."

"You haven't noticed it yet, but you do affect your surroundings. Have you noticed that you leave a trail of frost where you pass? Imagine if you can fully harness that power. And who really knows what other powers you have that haven't been discovered yet? That's why you must be protected until mama can win the battle."

"And if she can't beat Olena?"

"Then I pity mankind," said the cloud.

Mama/ Alona

I couldn't believe that Bosko had set me on fire. My entire body ached, but I tried not to think about it. I was far too old for my body to be this damaged. The cool concrete made my wounds feel better, but I knew I would have to get up and dress my wounds. I was so angry at Bosko. Why on Earth did he attack me like that? I wondered if Olena had said something to Bosko. She was such an evil child!

Groaning loudly, I began to sit up slowly. Patches of my burnt flesh stuck to the concrete as I began to stand up. I reached onto a small shelf to grab the basic first aid kit I had stashed in the war chamber. It didn't matter how much ointment I put on; the wounds looked pretty bad. Yellowish pus was leaking out of the blackened skin. Dried blood had made my skin sticky. I checked the time; I had called Nairobi almost two hours ago. Where was she?

There was a knock at the door. I pulled it open and beamed, "Finally, you are here!" Instead of Nairobi, it was a man dressed in all black. "Hello, Alona. Nairobi is currently dispatched to another location. I am here to help you. My name is Dimitri, and I am from the Russian division. Let's get you cleaned up." Dimitri was dressed in an expensive black suit and was taller than most men that I had seen in my life. Before she could answer him, he had pushed through the door and shut it behind him.

I could tell he was not like everyone else in the organization so I followed him without saying a word. I sat down on the concrete and leaned against the cool wall. I closed my eyes, and Dimitri sat down on the floor with me. "You shouldn't sit on the floor; you will ruin that expensive suit," I said, unsure of how to act. Dimitri laughed and shook his head. "I have thousands of these suits. You shouldn't worry about trivial things." His tone didn't match his eyes. In the dim light, he looked like a demon. I couldn't tell if I was just tired or if my mind was playing tricks on me.

He produced a vial that had what looked like green

slime. "You are going to drink this." He put the vial in my hands. "What is it?" I asked, unable to take my eyes off the substance in the vial. "I don't think you should ask something if you don't want to really know the answer. Just drink it. It will help you." Dimitri said as he took the cork out of the vial. He put my hand closer to my mouth. The vial smelled strangely of lavender. I took a deep breath and began to drink it as fast as possible.

It had a bitter aftertaste and made me start to gag. Dimitri sat there looking at me with an amused expression on his face. "You drank down something that will turn you younger." He had a smirk on his face that made him look a little older. The pain in my body began to erupt as I had just thrown myself into some lava. I tried desperately not to cry, but I could feel tears slipping down my cheeks. The veins in my arms were turning a bright red color, like my blood was on fire. I couldn't hold back my screams as I dropped to the floor. I was screaming like I was giving birth and couldn't stop. All the veins in my body were all bright red. My skin was stretched so tight around the bones of my body that I thought it would rip off my body. My vision got blurry, and my stomach felt like it was being ripped apart by razor blades. Dimitri sat there watching me with no emotion on his face.

My head was burning, and my hair fell out in giant clumps. Parts of my flesh on top of my head landed in my lap with the clumps of hair. My teeth fell out shortly thereafter. It felt like someone had taken a sledgehammer to my mouth. My gums were bleeding, and my tongue was raw. I was sobbing now, and it was hard to breathe. Just when I thought it wouldn't get any worse, it did. My teeth grew back in my mouth, and my hair grew on my head. Every bone in my body hurt as it snapped, then regrew back together. It felt like this transformation took hours when it only took about twenty minutes.

"Stay here and continue to heal. I will be back to check on you later." Dimitri smirked as he placed a bottle of water at my feet. He left without saying goodbye. I doubt I would have heard him because blood was coming from my ears. I closed my eyes, groaning loudly. "Oh my god, Alona! What happened to you?" Nairobi must have gotten here while I was busy "healing." I opened my eyes and pointed to the now empty vial on the floor by the water bottle. "Dimitri gave me this so I could heal and be younger." I managed to whisper. "Alona, did you just say Dimitri?" Nairobi asked, concerned. "Yes," I whispered as it felt like my organs were bursting inside of me. "Alona, Dimitri is not part of the organization. He is a rogue Charivyk. He was a sorcerer that got kicked out of the organization. He only helps people who have no chance of winning. He tricks people to drink water from a diseased swamp. Yes, it gives them an immortal body, but it gives the person brain worms. The brain worms will change a person according to their desires. If you were a hopeless romantic before you drank the potion, the brain worms would make you obsessive and a stalker. " Nairobi looked at me in horror.

I burped loudly and giggled. "I will be the same person I was before," I said, laughing uncontrollably. I was no longer in pain and could see how beautiful I looked. "I gotta call the organization to tell them what happened. Don't leave." Nairobi commanded me. I took a drink of the bottled water, and all the colors I could see became intensely amplified. It was too hot in the war chamber, so I waited until Nairobi turned her back, and I slipped outside. The air felt amazing, so I began to walk. I didn't know where I was going, but I wanted it to be as dark as possible. The light from the moon was hurting my eyes. I could hear Nairobi searching for me and calling out my name. I hid so she wouldn't find me and was trying so hard not to laugh out loud.

Ivan

Ivan wandered the forest. He took to trails he walked as a human and explored them in his new form. He hiked peaks and valleys in the Carpathians. He followed game trails and glided through brambles. He was enjoying the earth. It had a vibration he could feel in his soul. The vibration was soothing and rhythmic. Ivan rolled his head back and looked up at the stars. Even though it was high noon, he could see them. Clustered nebulas. Gas giants. He watched worlds form. He watched them die. Yet the earth remained calm. Ivan walked to the Bystrytsia River and stood at its banks. A movement in the water caught his attention. A whirlpool formed and grew. Debris from both banks was pulled into it. Discarded plastic bottles and other refuse were swept into its center, where it formed a shape. The shape grew straight up out of the center of the whirlpool. First, a torso made of logs, branches, and twigs. From the torso, two arms emerged. Ripping themselves free. They moved up the torso and dug into the top, and a head made from a trash can was freed. The canhead stretched and rolled around on its neck of thick vines. A mouth was formed from a rip in the cans side. Sharp metal teeth were visible in the shredded mouth. The mouth opened, and a grating voice howled to the heavens. The transformation was nearing completion as the creature walked to the bank of the river. Two eyes grinded open. More shrieking from that metal mouth, this time directed at Ivan, who stood there watching. The creature raised an arm and pointed a finger.

"I have been expecting you," it said.

Ivan felt the earth beneath his feet tense. It was as if the earth feared this creature's approach.

"Your journey is near complete," the creature said, "you will need to decide on your final allegiance."

"Allegiance?," said Ivan.

"You can only serve one master. Be it earth, wind, water, or fire. But only one."

"I serve no one," said Ivan.

"Oh, you will. Trust me," said the creature.

"And if I refuse," said Ivan.

"Refusal is not an option. This path you are on can only end up one way. You will become a most powerful ally. The Voda can reclaim the planet with your powers and abilities."

"Voda?" said Ivan.

"Voda. We are the water. The true life of this place. Nothing can exist without us. Nothing has ever happened without our involvement. We are eternity."

Ivan could feel the earth shift beneath his feet. It actually trembled. The earth was afraid of water that was clear.

The creature continued to grow as more debris was pulled into its wake. It now towered over the valley, getting stronger. Roaring, It swung an arm at a bank of trees and cut them down at their roots.

The earth split open next to Ivan, and a large rock was hurled at the creature, hitting it mid-sternum and tearing a hole through it. The creature roared again and thrust both arms into the hole the earth made. The creature dug furiously and widened the hole. Ivan could feel the earth's pain. Ivan saw the earth open up four more holes and watched the boulders as they were hurtled at the creature. Three hits to the sternum, making three more holes in it. The fourth bolder caught the creature under its chin, rocking its head back and knocking it off the torso. The creature, staggering now, flailed its arms wildly, cutting down trees and digging into the earth. The earth continued its rock barrage until the creature was once again a pile of river trash. The churning water where the creature stood began to settle as the remains of the creature were swept away. Ivan knelt down and tried to repair the damage caused to the earth by the creature. He did his best to fill the holes. He rose up and walked to the tree line where the creature did its most damage. Ivan put his hand on a shattered trunk and could feel the tree dying. It was calling out to its mother. Earth. Ivan could now sense the other trees and their suffering. He felt helpless. He turned back to the water. Choose a side, the water creature said. He did. Or so he thought until he ran into the fire.

Olena

I kept my eyes open for any new people I could lure with my dancing. This new location proved to be very lucrative. The bottom of my beloved lake was now filled with rotting skeletons. I didn't mind the smell anymore; in fact, I thought it smelled nice.

Nikolai kept groaning loudly, and it was irritating me. I thought of my father coming to visit me before he went to tell my mother he was leaving her. I hoped that went badly. I never thought of my mother in a bad way, but being a Mavka, I realized I hated her. I hated that she was so concerned about my every second of life. I hated that she ignored my brother, who only wanted her love when he was alive. I missed my brother a little bit. He was always around when I needed him. But deep down inside, I knew I couldn't trust him. In this war, he would choose my mother's side of things. He always did.

I wasn't going to lose this war, and there was no way I would be dragged to hell. My mother was so old, frail, and weak. I wasn't just going to destroy my mother, but the entire world would be mine. I smiled at that thought as I danced. Even after I died, I still felt pretty, and my dance movements were mesmerizing. I saw a woman approach the banks of my lake and smile at me. Curious, I swam up to her. "I can make your pain go away." I quietly sang. The woman smiled again, but she stepped closer to me this time.

"My name is Nairobi. I am actually here to help you. Your mother is now younger and stronger. You will need my help to win." Nairobi said as she offered her hand to me. I took it and enjoyed how warm it felt in mine. I began to pull her closer to me. I rose up from the water and gently kissed her lips which were done up with dark red lipstick. Nairobi smiled and sat down on the bank just centimeters from touching the waters.

"How is my mother younger?" I asked as I leaned on my elbows on the bank. Nairobi sighed loudly. Nikolai began to groan louder. "She was tricked and drank a potion. It transformed her into a younger, stronger version of herself. However, there is a major side effect she doesn't realize yet. She has to consume human flesh in order to keep her youth. If she consumes someone who is powerful, she will steal their powers." Nairobi said quietly.

"Ok, how do you expect to help me then?" I was getting bored with talking to Nairobi. Nairobi smiled and grabbed my arm. She pulled me almost out of the water. She grabbed my hand and placed it on her heart. "Aren't you hungry?" She smiled sweetly. I was, in fact, very hungry. It had been hours since I had devoured anyone. I looked at Nairobi to see her eyes change colors like my waters did when they lured someone to their deaths. I began to dig my nails into the soft, supple flesh of Nairobi's chest. Her flesh peeled to the side like it was made from paper.

Blood slowly dribbled out of the wound I made as I pushed aside the muscle tissues. Then I got to the chest plate. I cracked a bone from the chest plate and was surprised to see that Nairobi didn't blink. She sat there watching me with a smile on her face. I took the bone I cracked and ripped it out of her chest with a force. I sucked the bone marrow out of the broken bone that was in my bloody hands. It was the most delicious thing I had ever eaten in my entire life. I took the broken bone and stabbed at the heart of Nairobi. After several tries of positioning my hands better so they wouldn't slip with all the blood, I managed to rip out Nairobi's heart.

It was so dark; it was almost black in color. It was beating with a hypnotic rhythm. I watched as Nairobi dipped her hands into the lake and ran them over the gaping hole I left in her chest. To my surprise, the water didn't hurt her but healed her. I began to eat her heart like it was nothing but a chocolate-covered treat. It was delicious and sweet. It tasted like a holiday dish my mother used to make before the food strikes took away the ingredients to make. I couldn't remember the dish's name, but it was so savory. As I finished the heart, I could feel myself getting stronger.

My skin started to glow from the inside out. It was a strange feeling that was coursing in my veins. Everything started to smell sickly sweet to me. Nairobi stood up and straightened her belt. "Now, it will be an even match." She turned around for a second, paused, then turned back around. "You will need to convince Ivan to take your side. If he sides with your mother, you won't stand a chance. Ivan is incredibly powerful, and both sides are fighting for him." I was confused; how was Ivan so powerful? I wanted to ask Nairobi how I would locate Ivan, but she had disappeared.

My skin was beyond pale and seemed to be alive with a glowing light inside. I didn't feel much pain because, let's face it; I was no longer human. I began to dance slowly in the middle of the lake. I was fascinated with my body's light streaks as I began to dance. The light from inside of me made the waters look shimmery and full of magic.

The light in the water made the thousands of skeletons give off an eerie glow. It was so pretty to watch. "Hello, Olena." A voice sounded behind me. I twirled around gracefully and stood face to face with a woman I didn't recognize. She was a younger blonde woman. Her body looked odd and was proportioned in a weird way. Her eyes and breasts were the biggest part of her. Everything else was rail thin. She was pretty but wore too much makeup. "Who are you?" I asked her, watching her closely.

"Well, I am Dolores. Your father's mistress. Well, ex-mistress." She giggled. "Ok, so? Why are you here?" I was already tired of her presence. I couldn't care less that she used to sleep with my father. "I just wanted to tell you that I bankrupted your father. I left him homeless and penniless on the side of the road in the United States." She giggled again. Her giggle was annoying. It sounded like a duck being choked underwater. "I couldn't fucking care less," I said, surprising myself that I was using foul language. I guess being dead changed a lot about me.

"I am here for Nikolai." Dolores said as she inched closer to Nikolai. "Why? What do you want with him?" I asked as I swam closer to Nikolai. Dolores smiled, a smile dripping with sweetness and fakeness. "Because your family treated my family like dogs the entire time I worked for your father,"

Dolores said as she grabbed Nikolai's hand. I grabbed Nikolai's other arm. "You can't have Nikolai; he is mine." I hissed at her. She began to tug at Nikolai's arm. "I think you don't deserve him." She laughed. Everything about this woman was annoying me. "I don't think so. I suggest you leave." I said, rising up from the water. My eyes felt like hot pokers were emitting from them. Dolores grabbed Nikolai and began to pull him off the stick I had placed him on.

Screaming, I grabbed Nikolai's arm and gave it a good yank. His arm ripped off completely from the force of my yank. I tossed his arm to the side; I would eat it later. I grabbed Nikolai's leg as Dolores was able to yank him completely off the stick. His body slipped right out of my hands as he landed on the bank. Dolores picked him up and moved him away from the bank. Then she lit a cigarette and stared at me with hatred. "You don't get him." She said simply. Then she put her cigarette out on Nikolai's body. I watched as the man who pushed me into the lake and killed me rose in flames. I could hear his shrieks as the flames shot higher into the air.

Screaming, I dipped my hands into the lake and threw water onto Dolores. The water began to dissolve her body like it was made of nothing but salt. Within minutes, both bodies lay on the bank smoking. There was nothing left of Nikolai or Dolores. Just two bloodied piles of ash and smoke remained. I was alone. I couldn't stop screaming. I had never been so pissed off before. "Ivan! Get your ass here right fucking now!" I screamed over and over again. I didn't care that my foul language would definitely not call Ivan to me. I started to dance again, but this time I was thinking about how I would persuade Ivan to come side with me. How was I supposed to convince him to help me kill his mother, who he loved with all his heart when he was alive?

Ivan

High up in the Carpathian mountains, Ivan was sitting on the edge of a cliff. He surveyed the peaks and valleys below. The magnificent forest stretched for miles and miles. Rocks jutted out of the earth at impossible angles. He felt at peace. He could feel the gentle tug of gravity. He watched a turkey vulture make lazy circles in the air. He imagined himself riding the thermals. Ivan stood up and walked closer to the edge. The urge to fly was intense. Ivan wondered if he really could. Did his new powers include flight? He raised one foot and was about to leap out into the valley when a noise behind him made him turn. A mountain goat was walking towards him. Bold of him, Ivan thought. Most other forest creatures ran and hid from his approach. Not this goat. It walked directly towards him.

Ivan stood his ground and faced the goat. The goat seemed to ripple and shift as it continued its approach. Ivan eyed it cautiously as it stood up on its hind legs. It shifted again and let out a howl that caused all the birds in the valley to take flight.

The goat's hair fell out in bloody clumps, replaced by obsidian scales. Its face grew longer and its jaw sprouted jagged quartz teeth. The budding horns on its head grew into large ivory tusks. Cloven hooves on its hind quarters spread open flat, while its foreleg hooves splintered and grew seven fingers on each of its new hands. Finally, Ivan watched as the goat's eyes filled with smoke and burst. The flaming tears and fluids burning tracks on the goat's face. The empty eye sockets were replaced by two glowing red embers.

Another howl that Ivan felt in his soul. The goat's body grew in size and soon loomed over Ivan. Drool hanging from its gaping mouth. A whiplike forked tongue ran across a mouth full of razor-sharp teeth. Finally, it spoke.

"You are trespassing," said the goat.

Ivan said nothing.

"Don't you belong to the wind? Aren't you its new servant?"

Ivan said nothing.

"No need to hide it. We have been waiting for your arrival. You know that you are fulfilling a prophecy. For millennia, there was a balance between the elements. It grew boring. For every disaster, there was recovery. For every extinction, there was a rebirth. Since time immemorial. The one constant, you see, is the elementals. We have shaped this planet. We have cultivated and created. We have eliminated and exterminated. We have carved canyons in rock. We have moved continents. Until mankind, that is. Despite their frailty, humankind can be a handful. Deceitful, treacherous, spiteful, and destructive. They care little for this spinning rock. And as a result, some elementals want to eliminate mankind from this planet. Others want to nurture and develop these parasites. They didn't realize that by making them stronger, we doom our own existence. For a while, we thought we had a powerful ally in the retrovirus Covid-19. The wind really stepped up its game, spreading it. But the earth once again allowed mankind to heal itself. And now you come along. A new elemental. Your powers are still manifesting themselves, aren't they?

Ivan said nothing.

"I watched as you stood by and let earth battle water."

"It wasn't my fight," Ivan said, "my fight is with the creatures who stole my twin and changed her into a monster."

Ivan felt the earth shifting under his feet. It was as if the earth was trying to tell him something. Ivan tilted his head back and looked up at the goat. Its transformation was now complete; it was a formidable creature. He wondered if he could fight it. The earth lurched and shifted, and Ivan moved forward into the goat. The goat pulled back at Ivan's touch. Ivan noticed that just that light touch seemed to hurt the goat. Ivan reached his hand out to touch the goat again, but the goat was ready. It smiled as it burst into flames.

Ivan hesitated. He looked up at this ten-foot pile of burning rock and retreated back slightly. The goat spoke.

"Afraid of a little fire, boy?"

Ivan said nothing. He could feel the earth shifting again. This time moving him right and left. What was it trying to say?

The goat raised a hand and threw a fire bolt at Ivan's feet. The rock beneath Ivan's feet caught fire. The earth shifted. Ivan stayed put.

"Your precious earth is trembling," said the goat. It raised its hand again and threw more firebolts. They went to Ivan's right and left. Ivan was surrounded by flames. The earth trembled.

Ivan was finding it hard to see in all the smoke and flame. He could barely make out the goat still standing there, so he moved forward. Closer. The earth trembled.

"Brave little boy. Have you come to kneel before me and pay me tribute?"

"No," said Ivan, "I've come to extinguish you."

Ivan's body was raised up by the earth. He was now eye to eye with the goat. Ivan grabbed the goat by its throat. Flame lapped at Ivan's arms. It caressed his face as Ivan walked the goat to the cliff's edge. The goat was furious. It howled and squirmed in Ivan's grip. But Ivan's grip was vice tight. Ivan held the goat over the edge and lowered it so that Ivan could look down into its face.

"You haven't won. I will be back. Bigger and stronger. Remember that," said the goat as it twisted, freed itself from Ivan's grip, and fell into the valley.

Ivan watched as the goat bounced down the rocky mountain. He watched as pieces of black coal broke off the goat as it fell. The howling faded, and the goat was gone. Ivan turned back and began walking down the mountain. He neared a large boulder and noticed it change. Pieces of rock crumbled and chipped away from the boulder to reveal a large eye and an even larger mouth. The boulder spoke in a voice older than time.

"He will be back, you know. You haven't defeated him. He underestimated your powers. He won't make that mistake again."

"I hope he does. I know just the place for our next confrontation."

"You have made a powerful enemy. You must beware because he is Legion. He is born of fire and brimstone and has many forms."

"Then I can fight fire with fire,' Ivan said.

And he knew now how he could help mama. And, hopefully, save Olena's soul.

Alona

I felt so young! I hadn't felt like that in so many years. I wanted to do so many things now that I was young again. I ran for a long time keeping to the shadows until I found myself in a strange little village. When I was younger, my mother used to warn me of this village. "There are cannibals there, Alona." She had said it in such a manner of fact type of way. I was hungry, and the village carried an air of something delicious cooking. Without thinking about it, I followed the smell. My mouth was watering, and I made it to the edge of the village right before it was enveloped with a forest.

"You lost?" A man said behind me. I whirled around to see a man chiseled with immense muscles. "I'm hungry. It smells so good." I found myself saying as I wiped the drool forming in the corners of my mouth. The man looked me up and down with an intense stare. "You must be cursed." He said as he offered his hand to me. His fingertips were round, and his fingernails were bitten down to almost nothing. Somehow his gnarled fingers looked enticing. There was something magical about the way his fingers formed over mine.

He walked me to a big bonfire and sat me down on a comfy chair. "Another for dinner, a cursed one." He said to a man in a chef's hat. The chef smiled at me. I felt at ease for a second I forgot about Olena. The chef offered me a bowl with steam coming off it like a magic potion. Whatever the stew was, it was amazing. I had four bowls before I felt full. The man sat down beside me and wrapped his arms around me. "Hey, cursed one, that stew you devoured was made from a person. It would appear that if you don't eat people, your curse will destroy your body faster than you can blink. I suggest you stay here." His voice was so melodic I felt myself nodding. It didn't sink in what he said until that night when I fell asleep under the stars.

I was a cannibal. I had to be a cannibal to stay young. Olena. The name made me feel uneasy. I would have to destroy my daughter and drag her to hell. That thought left me feeling uneasy. I fell into a restless sleep, dreaming of Ivan destroying some sort of fire beast. I dreamt of Olena and I becoming one person. When I woke up, the sun was high in the sky, and I was hungry again. I would have to leave the only place I felt comfortable after I had some more stew to eat. I had to stop Olena before she destroyed the world. I ate the stew without thinking too much about the ingredients in it. I slowly chomped on an eyeball. It was crunchy at first, but then it burst into my mouth, leaking a very delicious juice into my mouth. Eyeballs had to be my new favorite thing to eat.

I began to write down my plan as I ate another bowl.

Olena

I was lonely, this luring people into my lake was becoming boring. Where was my mother? Wasn't she supposed to fight me or something? Drag me to hell? Where was Ivan? Why didn't he come when I called for him? Did he abandon me for some sort of adventure? I must admit, I was envious of him. I was glad he was finally living the life he deserved, but at the same time, I had hoped he would be by my side.

My little lake was so full of dead bodies and

skeletons that it was hard to dance around. Too bad I couldn't bottle up the lake and bring the fight to my mother. I couldn't say why I hated her so much. She never hit me or abused me in any way, but by the time I was a teenager, I hated everything about her. It was a deep hatred that festered like a rotting sore.

"Ivan!" I screamed at the top of my lungs. There was nothing but silence. I was truly alone. Sighing loudly, I picked up a rib cage and broke off a piece of bone. I was chewing on the tip of the bone when an idea hit me. I would make myself a water cage that would allow me to travel. I took skeleton after skeleton and began to fashion a cage that would hold my precious lake water and myself. It was time for the final showdown. Once I destroyed my mother, I would find Ivan. Some of the skeletons were slimy, so I was able to break those down into glue. It would take some time and look very morbid, but in the end, it made me excited. Hold tight, Ivan, I thought to myself. I am coming. I smiled and went back to fashioning the cage.

Ivan

During Ivan's trek back to the lake, he changed for the last time.

Earth
The Earth spun. Much as it always has. A little faster this millennia, not noticeable to its organic inhabitants, but faster nonetheless.
There was always peace between the earth and the

water. One could say that water was born from the earth. But, truth be told, water saved the earth.

Eons ago, the earth was still growing. Splitting and dividing. Land masses separated, creating huge caverns and canyons. Parts of the earth were still covered in molten lava that carved and shaped the earth the way He wanted. Since His birth, He wondered about His fate on this rock.

Fire. Born of combustion. Manifested in light, flame, and heat. Once the oxygen (thanks to the Air) became more plentiful, He grew in power. If He needs to be trapped on this huge piece of lava, He should rule it. So He fought the Earth, dominated it. Earth was not equipped to battle. Earth was gentle and nurturing. The fire took full advantage. So for millennia, the Earth just spun. A burning, molten, lava-filled rock, spinning without purpose.

Then one eon, the Wind changed. Constant heat caused small shifts in the currents that the Wind traveled. Funnels and drafts, and gales blew from all directions. Upper streams of air crisscrossed with lower dreams until one era, a cloud formed. The Wind was surprised by this, and when the cloud grew darker and darker, it seemed to burst into hardened fragments. The Earth noticed this too, and it also noticed as the cloud fragments tamed and cooled some of the molten rock.

The Wind was pleased with its changes. The Wind grew fond of the currents it carved in the Earth's atmosphere. Soon, the Earth was full of wind currents. The Wind helped cool the Earth, and it continued to produce clouds. And the clouds are who eventually helped the Earth tame Fire by having an offspring of its own, Water.

The first gathering of water took place high up on a mountaintop in a small crater. The Earth liked the feeling of this cool body sitting in its crater, and when the crater got too full to hold all the water, it spilled over the side and flowed down the mountain. Cooling hot rocks all along the way. The Earth noticed this and noticed how Fire had no defense against water. So the Earth formed a plan with Water. Fill my caverns and crevices. Fill my deep canyons with your coolness, and we can share this space. Fire tried its best to fight but retreated deep into the Earth's core. The balance was born. Earth, Wind, Water, and Fire would share this planet and its eventual spoils.

Alona

I wrote down my plans until my fingers started to bleed. The smell of blood made me hungry. I had to tell myself I couldn't sit there and keep eating. I needed to find my troublesome daughter Olena, the mavka. I looked around the small hut and found a leather-bound book carefully hidden within the slats of the walls. I pulled it out and saw that it had an eyeball on it. "One little snack won't hurt," I whispered to myself as I pried the eyeball carefully off the cover with my fingernail.

I did my best to savor the taste. It tasted way better than anything I had ever eaten before in my life and was gone too soon. I began to flip through the pages and read carefully the lettering that looked like it was produced from a bloody fingerprint. I realized my mistake almost instantly. The book I had in my hands was a powerful book that could make the living and immortal die. I had eaten the eye of death. I could hear a commotion outside. Carefully I put the book back in its hiding place and walked outside.

I could see Olena swimming around in a cage that looked like it was built from human bones. "I have found you, mother; let's end this! I am so fucking bored!" Olena had screamed at me. There was something about her voice that made me shiver. She no longer looked like my beautiful daughter. She looked like something you only see in horror movies. She started to sing, and I watched in horror as everyone in the village walked toward her cage. She grabbed each person and violently killed each person. Their bodies floated to the bottom of the shimmery water in her death-like cage.

I stood frozen in place. I forgot all that I was going to do. I couldn't take my eyes off the food floating in her cage. I couldn't shake the hungry feeling. My stomach was starting to hurt pretty badly. I looked down to see that some parts of my stomach had split open. I could blood in a couple of places that looked like someone had taken a knife to me.

"NO! Alona, don't go to her!" Someone yelled behind me. It sounded like maybe it was Dimitri or Nairobi. I couldn't tell; everything sounded distorted. I inched closer to the cage and looked at Olena right into her milky blue eyes. "Hello, mother, come closer. I have a tasty morsel for you to eat." She sang in such a pretty voice. For a second, I forgot that she wasn't my daughter. Her voice reminded me of my daughter when she was little.

I felt someone grab my arm and pull me backward away from the cage. I didn't want to stop listening to the pretty singing, and there was food. I was so hungry. I couldn't think of anything but to eat something. I leaned over slightly and took a big bite out of my arm. I could hear some distorted screaming, but I couldn't stop. I didn't taste too bad. I kept tearing at my arm, ripping through the tendons and muscles with my teeth. Some of my teeth chipped off into the tough tissue. When I got to the bone, I used my other hand and snapped it in half. I felt a stinging sensation briefly. One last bite, and I could rip my arm completely off my body.

"Don't eat that; I will come back for it!" I screamed but couldn't determine who was holding my severed arm. I ran up to the cage forgetting everything from my previous life. All I could focus on was getting into that cage to grab the meal that was making my mouth water. I started to snap the bones off of the cage and flung them behind me. "No, mama, stop!" I heard a voice call to me. But I could no longer remember having any children. I kept ripping at the cage until I could create a small enough hole to wriggle through. I jumped into the water and began to feast on the dead bodies floating. The water smelled bad, and I could tell it was melting off my skin. I didn't care; the water made everything taste good. The mavka that was singing swam up to me. She was screaming at me about something, clawing at my skin with long talons. She could shred through my bones as if they were made from the water I was now swimming in.

I grabbed her, and somehow, we both took a bite out of each other at the same time. She ripped out my heart, and I tore through her throat. She was delicious. She chewed on my heart. Things got murky for a little while. Things eventually cleared up, but we were no longer swimming in the water. We were standing at a fiery gate with an angry-looking man staring at us. "You were supposed to stop the mavka!" He screamed at me. Then he looked at her, and I realized that mavka was my daughter. I couldn't believe I had forgotten her in my hungry phase. "You were not supposed to be a mavka! Do you know what sort of imbalance you created?" The man was shouting and spraying red spit out of his mouth.

"Where's Ivan?" Olena asked. I sighed loudly; she was such a rebellious child. "Ivan is not coming here. He has found his purpose." The man screeched loudly. I realized I had failed my mission. Somehow, we both ended up in Hell. The man shoved Olena and me past the gate. The gate was burning, and he led us into a garden that was also on fire. Fire licked at my feet, and I started to scream. That hurt like Hell. We were led past the garden and into a room that was shaped like a triangle. He shoved us both into the triangle and then locked the door. The room itself was not on fire but filled with shimmery greenish-purple water. All we could do was float; we couldn't float near each other, or a fire would erupt somewhere on our bodies. I felt ashamed of myself that I failed. I tried to talk to Olena, but all she could was screech at me to shut up.

Olena

I glanced over at my mother, who looked like she was meditating. Why on Earth did she try to eat me? After all the legends she told me my entire life, I would have thought she would have known better. Now we are trapped in what I can only see as Hell. The water felt different than my lake; it felt more congealed. Like it was made from gel, it was soft and felt nice. However, every time I touched the sides, I got hurt. I was surprised I could feel the pain; it had been so long since I felt any pain at all.

My mother no longer looked like herself. She was younger, with her ribs sticking out. She looked like she had caught some sort of bug. Her eyes were no longer the color they used to be; they were completely void of color. It made her look haunted. I could see her slowly drag her arm through the gel-like water and try to chew on it. Was my mother really a cannibal? How did that happen? I didn't have the answers and wasn't sure I wanted them.

"IIIIVVVAAAAANNNN!" I tried to scream, but the gel-like water flowed down my throat and absorbed all the sound. Why wasn't he answering me? My voice could lure anyone. I wanted my brother to stand up to my mother finally. I wanted him to fight with me like we had when I was alive. Deep down, I knew that he wasn't coming back. Maybe he was living a good life in the afterlife. A part of me wanted that because he deserved happiness. The other part of me, however, was jealous. Sure, I got this cool Mavka thing going for me, but I felt more alone than I did when I was alive.

I made up my mind to escape, even if it took an eternity and messed up my body. I was going to leave my mother, who looked content enough to chew on herself. Very slowly, I began to force my way closer to the edge. It took a long time, and I got tired quickly. I took my long nail and began to scratch the triangle glass that kept me captive slowly. My fingernail peeled back to the flesh. Black sludge oozed out in replace of my blood. My blood seemed to wake my mother, and she began throwing her body into a slow-motion frenzy. Great, my mother really was a cannibal, and I was trying to escape. I couldn't afford any more mistakes. She kept trying to talk to me, but for some reason, her voice sounded like chainsaws cutting into metal. "Just shut up!" I muttered to her. I was sure she didn't hear me the gel-like water was clogging up my ears.

 I couldn't risk my mother reaching me and eating me before I could escape. I didn't know what would happen if she ate me, would she be eternally punished? Would we be reborn as one? I was tired of thinking of questions. I used another fingernail and started to scratch at the glass once more. I was going to break out one way or another. If I had to, I would eat my mother. The world hadn't seen the end of me. I belonged back on Earth and not in Hell. I didn't want to be reborn, and I didn't want to have to be punished. It wasn't my fault that I had turned into a Mavka.

Just like it wasn't my fault that I was born in the first place. If anyone needed to be punished, it was my mother. I would make sure she paid for everything she did. I would make her pay for not loving Ivan. As soon as I escaped, I would find Ivan and make sure he was happy.

A man appeared in front of the glass. "Ah, my two favorite people!" He clapped his hands loudly. My mother stopped chewing on her arm to look up. "I know you." She had screeched. The sound of her voice made the inside of my ears start to bleed. It was like blood in shark-infested water. My mother forgot all about the man standing in front of us and tried to move her body around to find where the scent of blood was coming from.

"Yes, Alona. I am Dimitri. I am the one who gave you the special potion. You should have listened to Nairobi. She is on the side of good. We had a little wager. I am so happy I won you both." Dimitri laughed heartily.

"Where is my brother?" I asked. My voice was hoarse, and I couldn't tell if the sound had cut through the water. "Ah, Ivan. Don't worry about Ivan. He is safe and is doing really well with his new role in life." He laughed again. His presence was pissing me off. My mother said something unintelligible. More black sludge-like blood gushed out of my ears.

"You won't escape, Olena. I know you're every thought and action before you do." He waved his hand in front of my face, and suddenly black rings appeared on my wrists and ankles. The rings started to burn intensely. "I will prove you wrong," I whispered as I glared at him. My mother returned to chewing on her arm, and the man left. I could see dark reddish-purple welts from under my skin where the rings touched. Maybe I should have my mother eat them off of me. I laughed. I wasn't going to think a single thought, and I was going to prove that man wrong.

The End

9 7 9 8 3 6 3 6 4 6 4 1 6